To my Bernadette,
For the ant and the love of summer.
M.-H. J.

To my love Dahlia.
A. D.

NOTHING AT ALL!

Written by **Marie-Hélène Jarry**
Illustrated by **Amélie Dubois**

SIMPLY READ BOOKS

Today I am a lazy lizard.
A lazy lizard dreaming on its back, belly to the sun.

I am counting the clouds: there are three of them!
Three big snails in the sky.
I am lying on the grass.
I am not moving.

Out of the corner of my eye, I notice Daddy.
"Hey, Clara, what are you doing?"

I answer, "Nothing! I'm looking at the clouds."
He looks at me, and then at the sky, and returns
to the kitchen.

I close my eyes.
All I hear is
the tap running.
With no wind, the trees are silent.

I hear Daddy again.
"Clara, what are you are you doing?"
"Nothing. I'm listening to the trees."

He asks, "Why don't you go
to the pool with Léa?"
I picture Léa and the others
splashing and yelling.
"No, *please*, Daddy! I want to stay here."
He does not insist.

The grass is soft. An ant tickles my arm with its little steps.
I place it on a blade of grass.

Do ants ever stop running?

I can feel Daddy's footsteps on the ground.
He is very near. "What's wrong, Clara?"
"Nothing! I'm just trying to stay still."

"Sure, but it's a magnificent day
for a bike ride!"
The phone rings.
Daddy runs to take the call.
Whew!

The garden smells like lavender
and cut grass.
A piece of dandelion fluff lands on my nose.
It makes me sneeze.

Daddy comes back, along with the smell of tomato sauce.
"Clara, are you sulking? What are you thinking about?"
I explain again, "Nothing, Daddy! I'm breathing in the flowers."
"Oh, really... Why don't we bake muffins?"
Poor Daddy, he doesn't understand.
He leaves.

Daddy would like me to be busy from morning to night.
But today, doing nothing
is exactly what I want to do!

Rémi isn't so lucky.
He always has a lesson for one thing or another.

When we have nothing to do,
we can think about whatever we want.
I discover a marvelous world
with Alice and the Little Prince.
I tell myself jokes
and I laugh to myself.
I can also think about
nothing at all!

Thinking about nothing
is so relaxing.
But what *is* nothing?
An enormous hole in the middle of nowhere?
Or is it an immense, empty sky?
I imagine myself floating in infinite space.
There are no more sounds; no one bothers me.
It is so soft, so mellow, so...

I open my eyes.
The shade has reached across the garden.
It's so late!
Leaning over me, Daddy softly says,
"Did you sleep well? It was cute. You were smiling..."

All of a sudden it comes back to me.
"I was dreaming about nothing. It was beautiful."

Daddy chuckles and shakes his head. "You did look very peaceful."
He is about to sit next to me in the grass, when the smell of
fresh-baked muffins drifts from the kitchen,
and he has to go see if they are ready.

Still, I don't move.
I will go taste the delicious muffins
when Daddy has finished with his bowls, his pans and hubbub.

Then maybe we will sit together, doing nothing.

Published in 2021 by Simply Read Books
www.simplyreadbooks.com
Text © 2016 Marie-Hélène Jarry
Illustrations © 2016 Amélie Dubois

Library and Archives Canada Cataloguing in Publication

Title: Nothing at all! / written by Marie-Hélène Jarry ; illustrated by Amélie Dubois.
Other titles: Rien du tout! English
Names: Jarry, Marie-Hélène, 1954- author | Dubois, Amélie, 1979-, illustrator.
Description: Translation of: Rien du tout!
Identifiers: Canadiana 20200303082 | ISBN 9781772290271 (hardcover)
Classification: LCC PS8569.A69 R5313 2021 | DDC jC843/.54—dc23

Originally published in French in 2016 by les Éditions de l'Isatis, as Rien du tout!

We gratefully acknowledge for their financial support of our publishing program the
Canada Council for the Arts, the BC Arts Council, and the Government of Canada.

Manufactured in Korea

10 9 8 7 6 5 4 3 2 1